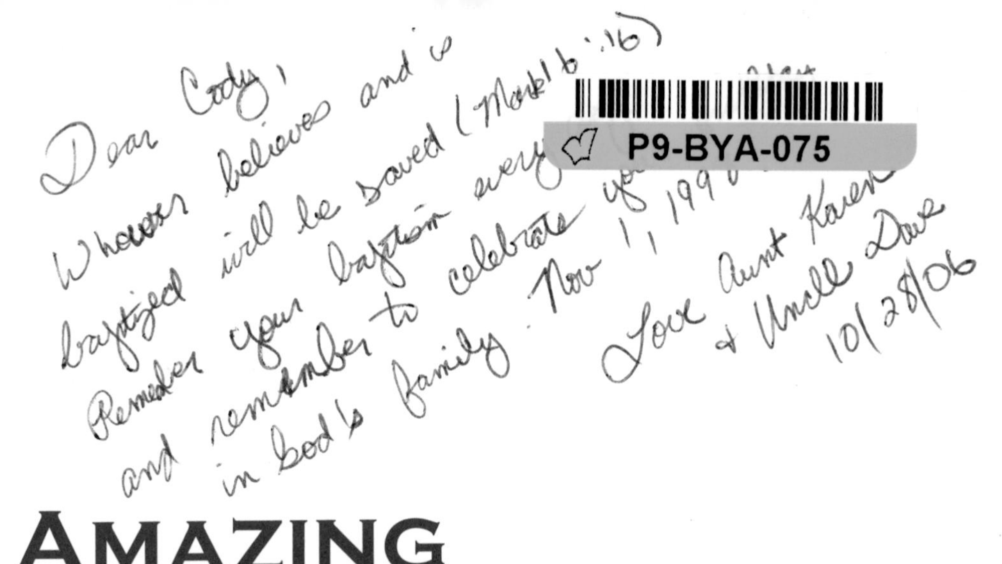

# Amazing & Unexplainable Things in the Bible

# AMAZING & UNEXPLAINABLE THINGS IN THE BIBLE

WRITTEN BY
RICK OSBORNE
ED STRAUSS

ILLUSTRATED BY
JACK SNIDER

Zonderkidz

Zonderkidz®

*The children's group of Zondervan*

www.zonderkidz.com

Creepy Creatures and Bizarre Beasts from the Bible

Requests for information should be addressed to:
Grand Rapids, Michigan 49530

---

**Library of Congress Cataloging-in-Publication Data**

Osborne, Rick.

Amazing and unexplainable things in the Bible / Rick Osborne, Ed Strauss.

p. cm.

Summary: Explores miracles mentioned in the Old and New Testaments and why they are amazing, and suggests how the lessons of these inexplicable events can be applied to one's daily life.

ISBN 0-310-70653-X (pbk.)

1. Miracles--Biblical teaching--Juvenile literature. [1. Miracles. 2. Christian life.]
I.Strauss, Ed, 1953- II. Title.

BS680.M5O73 2004

220.6'1—dc21

2003010759



*Editor: Gwen Ellis*

*Art direction & interior design: Michelle Lenger*

*Printed in U.S.A.*

04 05 06 07/RRD/5 4 3 2 1

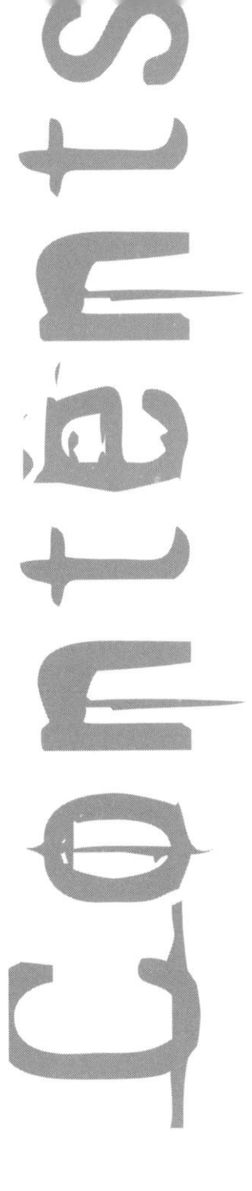

## Miracles, Signs, and Wonders

Fire from the sky, a sun that refuses to set, the dead coming back to life, angels battling armies, farmers performing feats of supernatural strength, and much, much more! The Bible is full of amazing signs, wonders, and miracles! Why are they in the Bible? Is it just for special effects, as in some Hollywood blockbuster? Do you ever wonder, "Why does God do wonders? Why miracles?" And what does it mean to say, "God, give me a sign"? Is that like asking him to paint a poster for your youth group's fund-raiser?

A *sign* is a miracle God uses to get people to pay attention. When Moses needed people to believe that he was God's prophet, God caused his wooden rod to morph into a snake. *That* was a sign! You bet all eyes were glued to it! Jesus also did miraculous signs so people would pay attention and take his words seriously—and find eternal life (Mark 16:20).

The words *signs* and *wonders* and *miracles* sometimes mean the same thing, but they also have their own very interesting meanings. For example, when Jesus and the apostles performed miracles, often the word *miracle* (from the Greek word *dunamis*) means "an act of power." *Power!* Yeah! Now we're talkin'!

*Wonders* means, well, something wonder-full—full of wonder. But often *wonders* means the same thing as *miracles.* That is, after all, one of the main reasons for miracles: to get people to wonder about God's wonderful power. Like the time Jesus healed a crippled man, and the crowd was "filled with awe . . . and they praised God" (Matthew 9:8).

Sometimes God does miracles to teach his people that he loves, cares for, and protects them. This lesson was really hammered home when God parted the Red Sea so the Israelites could escape the Egyptian army. The Israelites didn't have the time to build rafts. They didn't have three million surfboards to paddle out on. But God showed them that with him on their side, they didn't need to worry.

God provided the Israelites with a miraculous food called *manna*. It showed up six days a week on the ground outside their tents. Why did God do it this way? Well, his people needed food, and this was an excellent opportunity to show them—and all future generations—that he could meet their needs.

Signs, wonders, miracles? God has lots of reasons for doing things in a big, splashy, special effects kind of way. But the main reason is so we can see what he's like and learn to trust him to care for us and love us. Sometimes God cares for us in small, seemingly natural ways. You know, the kind of miracle where you say, "Hey, I asked God about that and then it all worked out!"

We hope you have lots of fun reading about miracles, signs, and wonders. And while you're at it, we hope you learn something about what God is like and how he can work in your life.

## Extra! Extra! God Creates Planet Earth

Some people can't imagine God creating everything in six days (Exodus 20:11). That means the entire earth, the seas, the mountains, the animals, and the plants in only 144 hours. That's about three seconds to design and put together an elephant, one second for a mosquito, and so forth. *However!* When you think of how infinitely powerful and wise God is, the amazing thing is that he didn't create *everything* in three seconds! You know what multitasking is, right? It's when your mom does three things at once? Well, God can multi-multi-multi-multitask. Think about it. He can hear and answer everyone who is praying all around the world—*and* run the whole universe—at the same time. It probably wouldn't have been a big deal for him to build an elephant and a mosquito at the same time.

## OH . . . HE *ALSO* MADE THE UNIVERSE

On day four God wanted lights in the sky, so he created the sun and moon. Then the Bible says, "He also made the stars" (Genesis 1:14–16). It wasn't as if God said, "Whew! I spent the entire day making one sun and one little moon. I've got a few minutes left; why not make all the galaxies full of mega-billions of stars?" No, day four was Galaxy Day. The sun and the moon were part of the whole shebang. Our Milky Way Galaxy contains more than one hundred billion stars, and there are billions of galaxies like ours in the universe! Think of how *huge* God must be to make everything!

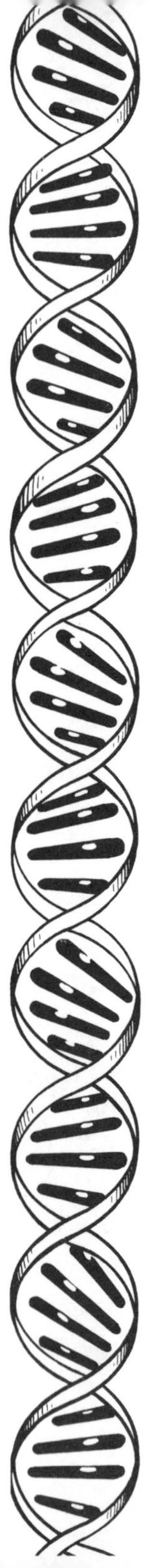

## Life's DNA Blueprint

The blueprint for all plant and animal life is found in its tiny DNA helix. Every part of a Venus flytrap—from its dew production to its fly-gobbling digestive system—was written in its DNA. As incredibly small as human DNA is, every bit of information on how to form arms, legs, lungs, hearts, and brains is written in it. And did you know that all the information about your entire body is in one itsy-bitsy, tiny cell in a flake of your skin? Each cell is made up of DNA, and each DNA helix is made up of molecules, and molecules are made up of atoms, and atoms are made up of electrons, protons, and neutrons, and protons and neutrons are made up of even smaller particles called quarks. God made all these details.

## Guy from Dirt, Girl from Rib

God said, "Let the land produce living creatures" and it did. Then God created Adam from dirt, too. But when it came to Eve, dust just wouldn't do. God took one of Adam's ribs and made a woman from it. (See Genesis 1:24; 2:7, 21–22.) Was this the world's first cloning? DNA engineering? The first order for take-out ribs? No, it was just a weird miracle. That's right: girls are weird miracles. Seriously, however, humans are truly amazing! Grab an encyclopedia about the human body, and you'll be amazed at how our billions of cells work together. Our nervous system, digestive system, and all the muscles, bones, and organs are so complicated and mysterious that science is still scrambling to understand them.

## God-Made Instincts

When God created people and animals, he gave them instincts. Doing things by instinct means you do them without thinking. The desire to guzzle down a huge glass of fluid after a hot day skateboarding is an instinct. God hardwired that desire right into your brain.

It's the same with animals: God didn't just make them different on the outside. He wired them differently on the inside as well. Read Proverbs 30:24–28 to see how God made ants to be naturally organized, or how coneys (rock badgers) instinctively know where to build homes. God gave different animals unique instincts. For example, he didn't give your cat the instinct to swim furiously upstream in a raging river. That's salmon stuff. He didn't give dogs the instinct to build nests in trees. That's a bird thing.

Speaking of birds, God put the migration

instinct in lots of bird brains. They wake up one morning, it's cold, they look at each other, ruffle their feathers, maybe shiver a bit, shake a leg, then they just take off and fly thousands of miles to spend winter in the warm South. Jeremiah said, "The stork in the sky knows her appointed seasons, and the dove, the swift and the thrush observe the time of their migration" (Jeremiah 8:7). Though they don't know how they know, they know it's time to go.

God made people warm-blooded: we stay more or less the same temperature all day. He made reptiles cold-blooded. So how do snakes warm up? Simple. Rocks soak up heat fast, so snakes slither on top of sunshiny rocks to get all toasty. God told them to do that (Proverbs 30:18–19). "Cold? Get yourself up on that rock, buddy."

Q: Why didn't Adam and Eve play board games?

A: They lost their pair o' dice (paradise).

God puts *spiritual* instincts in people, too—he gave us a deep instinct to seek spiritual things. Ecclesiastes 3:11 says, "He has also set eternity in the hearts of men." God gave us a conscience to instinctively know the difference between right and wrong. "The requirements of the

law are written on their hearts" (Romans 2:15). Instincts? Yeah, they're cool stuff.

# GET SMARTER

**Solomon, one of** the smartest guys who ever lived, said that the fear of God was the beginning of wisdom (Proverbs 1:7). Solomon knew a lot about God and life. He learned those things when he studied creation—the plants and animals God had made. Solomon's key to figuring things out was to start with God. His first assumption was that God made everything and that he made things to serve his purposes. Solomon realized that everything God made came from his heart and therefore you could learn about God's character by studying nature. Want to be smart? Then remember that God made everything you'll ever learn about in life.

## God Unbolts Chariot Wheels

When the Egyptian army was chasing the Israelites through the Red Sea, God "made the wheels of their chariots come off so that they had difficulty driving." Um, yeah, that would make driving difficult.

*Whumpity-clangity-thumpity-whump-whup!*

"Hey, Nefu! Our chariot just became a sled!"

"Do you have a spare in the back?"

"Make that 599 spares! Look! The wheels came off all the other chariots as well!"

"Whoa! Wheels rolling past! Watch out!"

*Cluuungg!*

It must've been like the inside of a pinball machine.

Then the Red Sea fell on top of them. Well, if *that* wasn't just peachy! It *was*, for the Israelites . . . but for the Egyptians? Just the night before, the Israelites were complaining because they were trapped between the Egyptian army and a sea. A day or so later they'd seen God:

- hold back the army with a pillar of fire
- make a path through the sea
- remove chariot wheels
- wipe out their pursuers

God taught the Israelites that they didn't need to worry or complain when he was on their side. (See Exodus 14:21–28.)

## Up, Win—Down, Lose

When the Israelites camped at Rephidim, some mad nomads called Amalekites attacked. Moses stood on a hill, watching the battle, giving his troops the "high ten" by holding his staff up in both hands. At first the Israelites were winning, but whenever Moses became tired and lowered his hands, the nomads began winning. All day long, up, down, up, down. Win, lose, win, lose. Aaron and Hur finally got the connection and held up Moses' hands till sunset. And the Israelites won. (See Exodus 17:8–16.) They were just starting to do battle for God, and this win helped them see that God was fighting for them.

## Deuteronomy's Durable Duds

When God reminded the Israelites what he'd done for them in the desert, he said, "Your clothes did not wear out . . . during these forty years" (Deuteronomy 8:4). That was some laundry miracle! Think! If the knees in your blue jeans never wore out and your favorite T-shirt stayed new-looking, you'd never have to change them. *Cool!* And you'd never have to buy new clothes. That would drive girls crazy but it'd be great for boys! God probably didn't even tell the Israelites ahead of time that he was going to do this. He just went about the business of caring for his people.

## Fire Vaporizes Stone!

Breaking news from the God-Baal showdown on Mount Carmel today. Well, we definitely have a winner, and the results are: *God is God!* Baal came in a disappointing second, and . . . well, actually, Baal didn't come in at all. He was a no-show. Elijah joked that Baal must be sleeping or off on a trip. Or, like, nonexistent. Whatever Baal's pathetic excuse, he couldn't set fire to his sacrifice. God, on the other hand, sent down a fire bolt as hot as the surface of the sun. As you will recall, the question was, "Can you set the sacrifice on fire?" God not only burned the wood *and* the bull but vaporized the water, dust, and altar stones! (See 1 Kings 18:20–38.)

## Antigravity Axhead

A company of prophets decided to build a house, so they began chopping down trees in the Jordan River Valley. One guy swung a little too hard and the iron axhead—*plooop!*—disappeared in the muddy river. Iron tools were super-expensive back then—like, about the price of a signed Wayne Gretsky rookie card in mint condition—so this prophet was in big trouble. But not for long. Elisha cut a stick, chucked it in the water, and "made the iron float." (See 2 Kings 6:1–7.) This is not as easy as it sounds. Try it, you'll see. The stick didn't have the power to raise the axhead. If floating wood could make sunken metal float . . . *wow!* Just throw a few logs in the ocean and up would come the *Titanic*! What did the job was Elisha's faith.

## Tonight's Song Is "Chariots and Armies"

God has one humongo speaker system. One night he decided to play a marching tune full blast. The Aramean army was camped around the city of Samaria, so God "caused the Arameans to hear the sound of chariots and horses and a great army." The soldiers were so scared, they ran off. (See 2 Kings 6:24; 7:3–7.) It makes you wonder what *other* sound effects God has up there. How would you like to hear your favorite CD played on that sound system?

## Iron Gate Opens Itself

When the angel sprung Peter out of prison, he led him into the outer courtyard and up to the huge iron gate. Locked, of course. The angel didn't touch the gate. He didn't need to. The gate was on their side. "It opened for them by itself." (See Acts 12:6–11.)

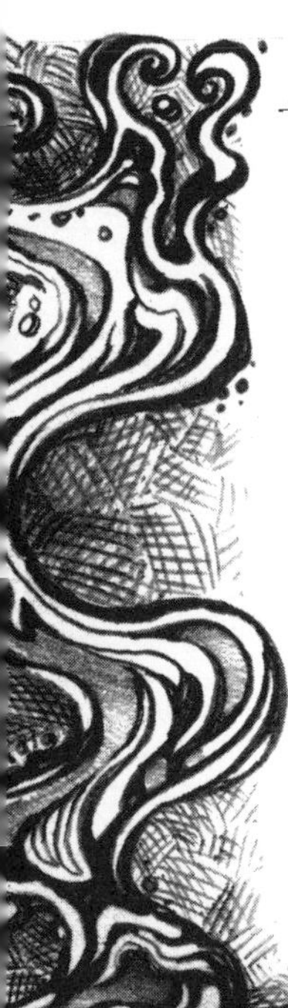

GET STRONGER

**So what do** you need? The local bully to leave you alone? The watch you lost in the meadow to be found? The door to somehow open when you're locked out? Help getting the campfire started? More clothes? Lift your hands up as Moses did and ask God for help. Don't try to tell God how to answer your prayers, though. After reading the last stories, you can see he likes to do things in creative ways. So give him some elbowroom.

### You Just Won a Forty-Year Supply!

About three million Israelites were in the desert for forty years, and during that time they ate manna three times a day—not including snacks. That's a *lot* of manna! Every person ate one omer (two quarts) of manna per day (Exodus 16:21–22). So how much manna did that crew chow down in forty years? To get a ballpark figure, multiply three million people times forty years times 365 days times two quarts, and you get nearly ninety *billion* quarts of manna (87,600,000,000 to be exact). Let's hear a big old *burp!*

### What Was Manna?

Every morning, except on Saturdays, there on the ground outside the Israelites' tents was the manna—

white and looking like resin (Numbers 11:7). They asked, *"Manna?"* (Hebrew for "What *is* it?"). Some people think it was sap that oozed out of tamarisk trees. Problem is, tam-sap can't be eaten and can't be cooked. *Bwaaaap!* Wrong guess. Okay, okay, so it must've been sticky gobs of insect body fluids. What? Eating bug gloop for forty years? Was that why the Israelites complained, "Now we have lost our appetite" (Numbers 11:6)? No. Sinai insects only excrete goo in June, not all year round. So that wasn't it. Think: if it were just something natural like bug goo or sap, then why, once a week faithfully, every Saturday, would it *stop* oozing? 'Cause it was a miracle! The bread of heaven (Psalm 105:40)!

## It's Raining Big Fat Birds!

When God told Moses that he was going to give the Israelites meat, Moses asked, "Would they have enough if all the fish in the sea were caught for them?" Surprise, surprise, fish was not on the menu. (Though God could have rained fish on them if he had wanted to.) Instead . . . *Flappity-flap-flap! Whap! Whap! Thump!* "Look! Millions of quail are flopping all over camp." Every person caught at least ten homers of quail (about sixty bushels), which altogether is 180 million bushels of quail. (See Numbers 11:18–23, 31–32.) Let's see . . . how many different ways can you cook quail? It must've been like turkey after Thanksgiving: turkey sandwiches, turkey leftovers, turkey pot-pie, turkey soup . . . you get the picture.

## Ravens: "On *Today's* Menu . . ."

One day the prophet Elijah stormed in to tell King Ahab and Queen Jezebel that God would send a drought on the nation as punishment for their sins. This made Ahab and Jezzy *vewwwy* mad, so Elijah ran to Cherith Creek and hid out. Good idea, Elijah. Yeah, except for *one* minor detail: there's no *food* there. Hey, not a problem! Every day, twice a day, God ordered ravens to snatch food off people's tables and, with the eats in their beaks, to fly out into the wilderness and feed Elijah.

## Refills on Flour and Oil

From the beachside city of Zrephath comes a story that takes the cake—literally. There was a terrific famine, but for three years a widow, her son, and the prophet Elijah ate cake every day. However, all she had to bake with for three years was one handful of flour and half a cup of oil! Wow! How did she make it last so long? Well, one day Elijah showed up, and when she unselfishly shared her last bit of food with him, God made the flour and oil replenish itself. She kept using up the food, but every time she went to cook the next meal, there was more flour and oil. (See 1 Kings 17:8–16.)

## Stick Sweetens Water

When the Israelites crossed the Sinai Desert, they found water at Marah. Only one problem: the water was bitter. "Pah! Yuck!" They couldn't drink it. Moses prayed, saw a stick, and—*plop!*—threw it in the water. ("Oh sure! Like *that's* gonna help!" Well, it *did*.) The water became sweet. Not like ice cream but sweet as in "not bitter." (See Exodus 15:22–25.) Does this mean you can throw a stick in your spinach? Probably not. It only worked because that's what God told Moses to do.

### Killer Water Tamed and Tasty

When Elisha went to Jericho, the people complained, "The water is bad."

"Like, *how* bad?"

"Well, it causes death."

"Mmm, that *is* bad."

So Elisha got a new bowl, filled it with salt, then threw the salt in the spring. And from that day on, the water stopped killing people. Was it miracle salt? No. God did the miracle. (See 2 Kings 2:19–22.)

## Olive Oil Miracle!

One day a prophet, who was in debt, died. Since his widow had no money, the creditor threatened to grab her two sons as slaves. When Elisha heard that all she had in her house was a little olive oil, he had her borrow all her neighbors' jars. Okay? Now start pouring oil. Huh? Her boys kept lugging jars and she kept pouring. Finally she ran out of jars. Then the oil stopped multiplying. The widow sold all the oil, returned the jars, and paid her debts. (See 2 Kings 4:1–7.) This was probably one chore that her boys never whined about. "Well, boys, you can either help out or be sold as slaves." Wouldn't *you* be motivated?

## New Cook's Helper Needed

One day in Gilgal, the prophet Elisha opened a soup kitchen for a hundred hungry prophets. He put on a large pot of stew, but the cook's helper diced up a no-name gourd and poisoned the meal. Apart from learning to be careful about whom they let in the kitchen, the

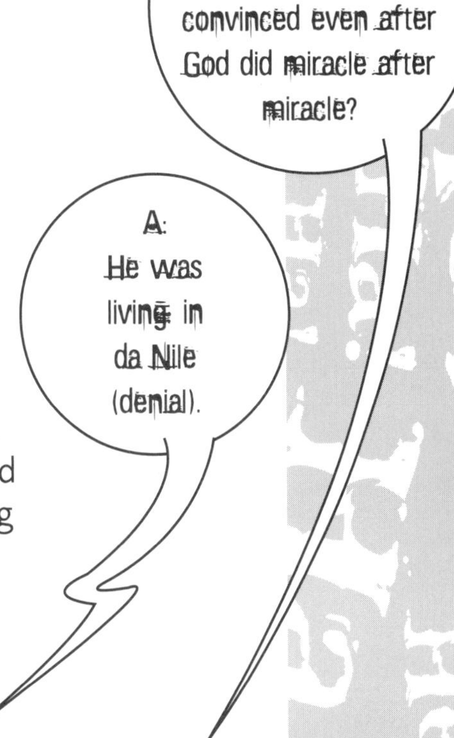

prophets learned that God still performs miracles. Elisha threw a handful of flour into the pot and—voilà!—"Compliments to the chef and the miracle-working God." (See 2 Kings 4:38–41.) You may not have eaten poison stew, but moldy fridge leftovers can make you sick as a dog, too!

## Bread for One Hundred

Same famine, same one hundred prophets, but now the stew pot's empty. Along comes a man with twenty loaves of barley bread. Elisha says, "Give it to the people to eat." Twenty little loaves for a hundred big men? Let's do the math: that's one-fifth of a loaf per guy—like, about half a bun each. Elisha repeats, "Give it to them," so his servant gives it to them. The bread miraculously multiplies, the guys eat and eat, and they even have some left over (2 Kings 4:42–44).

## Way, Dude! Lotsa Food!

Samaria was besieged by the Aramean army, which meant that they had the city surrounded and no one got out or went in. Food became so scarce that people were paying eighty shekels of silver for a donkey's head. Elisha was in Famine City, too, and when he told the king that the next day there'd be tons of food to eat, the king's right-hand man basically said, "No way!" And Elisha basically replied, "Way. You'll see it, dude, but you won't taste it." That night God scared the willies out of the Arameans. They ran off so fast, they left their horses and donkeys behind. You're probably thinking the people ran out and ate all the *donkeys*, right? You would be wrong. The Aramean camp was loaded with wonderful food. Do you remember Mr. No Way? Well, when the people stamped out the gates to grab some grub, Mr. No Way got in the way and was trampled. (See 2 Kings 6:24–25; 7:1–7, 16–17.)

## Jesus Does It Again!

Elisha fed one hundred men with twenty barley loaves. Pretty cool. But when Jesus came along, he broke the bread and broke the record. Talk about miracle power! First he fed a crowd of five thousand men (plus women and children) with only five loaves and two fish. A while later he fed another four thousand men (plus women and children) with seven loaves and a few small fish! (See Mark 6:34–44; 8:1–10.) Total? Including women and children,

Q: Which was the longest-lasting miracle in the Bible?

A: When God provided the Israelites manna in the desert for 40 years. (Exodus 16:35).

Jesus fed about twelve thousand people with twelve loaves and six little fish. You do the math on that: that's one loaf for every one thousand people, and one fish for every two thousand people. Yet everybody was full, and there were more loaves and fish left over than what they had started with!

## GET DEEPER

**At one point** when Jesus was feeding and healing the crowds, he realized that many of the people were just coming for dinner and a show. We are God's children and he loves us. He loves to take care of us and meet our needs, but that's not supposed to be the end of it. How would you feel if your friends hung around you only because you brought candy to school?

Pray for the things you need, sure, but also just to spend time with God. Talk to him about everything, not just about the things you'd like.

# HOW DID HE DO THAT?

Some people don't believe miracles can happen. They only believe in natural forces like gravity, electricity, and the Internet (just kidding). They think nothing can go against the laws of nature. But hey, you gotta understand, God is the one who set up those laws. He not only knows how they work, but he knows how to type in fresh commands to make them do cool new stuff.

That floating axhead, for example. Gravity is a natural law that works 24/7. It's what makes you land on the sidewalk when you wipe out on your skateboard. It's also what keeps your school bus from drifting off into outer space. Under normal circumstances no heavy iron axhead at the bottom of a river is gonna float up to the surface—unless God puts a little *anti-gravity* to work. Which he apparently did.

We don't understand God's power, but it's real—as real as electricity or splitting the atom. Plug into God and you can do cool things. Like when God anointed Jesus with the Holy Spirit and *power* (Acts 10:38; Luke 5:17). It doesn't matter that the smart boys down in Houston can't figure out the mathematical formulas for that. God's power works and that's all that matters. God himself put it this way: "I am the

LORD, the God of all mankind. Is anything too hard for me?" (Jeremiah 32:27). Some things are impossible? For *you*, maybe. But "what is impossible with men is possible with God" (Luke 18:27). God is a supernatural being. He's all-powerful and he can do anything. He made this world and everything in it in a mere six days.

We're governed by the natural laws he made, but it's silly to say that because God made nature and natural laws, he now is limited to only doing things naturally. That's like saying that because you set up an aquarium and put fish in it, you must now spend the rest of your life in the bathtub. God made natural laws to keep us safe, but he is still supernatural. In a way, we too aren't limited to natural laws, because we have a supernatural heavenly Father who loves us. "Everything is possible for him who believes" (Mark 9:23).



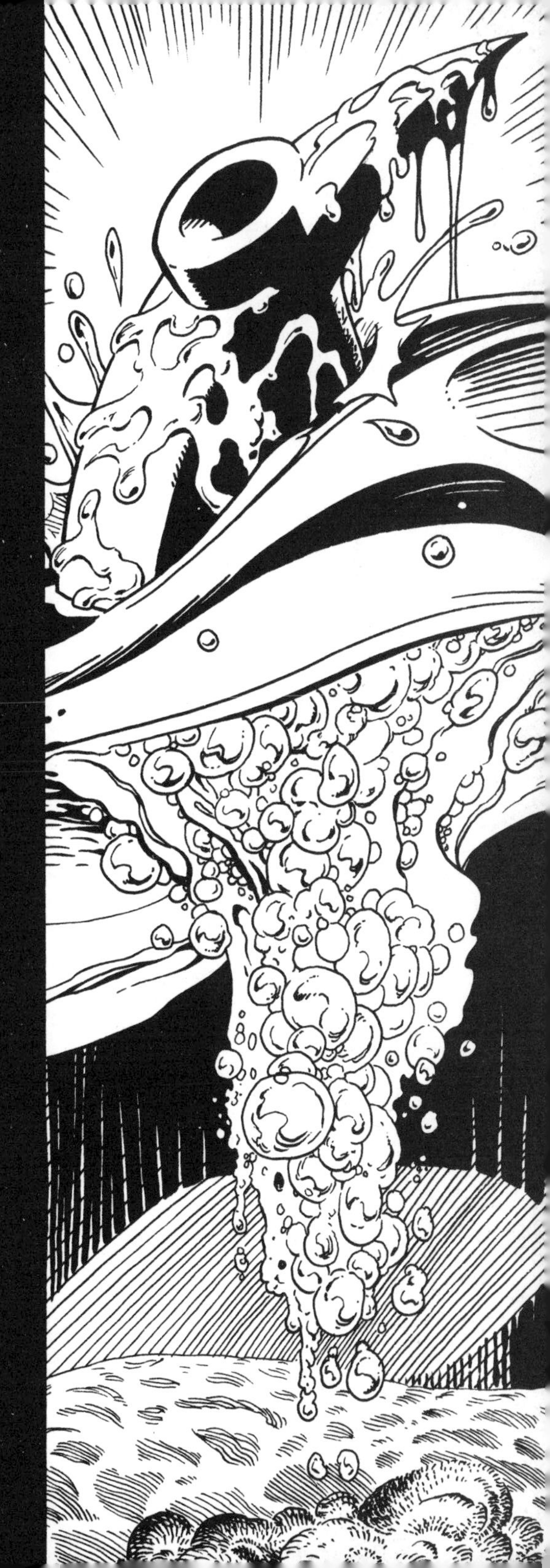

## Weather as a Weapon

It may not seem fair—if you were on the other side—but God often used weather as a weapon, particularly hailstones and lightning. "The Lord thundered. . . . He shot his arrows and scattered the enemies, great bolts of lightning and routed them." (See Psalm 18:12–14.) God also keeps snow, wind, and rain handy "for days of war and battle." No human has that power. God asked Job, "Do you send the lightning bolts on their way?" (See Job 38:22–23, 35.) "Welllll . . . no."

Don't get the wrong idea, though. Insurance companies refer to natural disasters (such as weather disasters) as "acts of God." That's not necessarily true. God set up the world's weather systems and patterns, but creation itself was corrupted by the effects of sin (Romans 8:20–21). So we ended up with weeds, diseases, and messed-up weather. When God wants to intervene and change the weather, he can do it. But otherwise the insurance companies should call them "acts caused by sin in the world."

## *DRY* WEATHER A WEAPON, TOO

Sometimes God sent a drought and it didn't rain for years. Moses warned the Israelites that if they turned from the Lord, God would strike with "scorching heat and drought. . . . The LORD will turn the rain of your country into dust and powder; it will come down from the skies until you are destroyed" (Deuteronomy 28:22–24).

"King! King! It's raining!"

"Finally! Whoopee! I'm just gonna run out in the rain, tilt my head back, and . . .

*Ackk! Cough!* "Hey! This is a *dust* storm."

"Yeah, well, rain ain't what it used to be."

## Worst Storm in Egypt's History!

When Pharaoh refused to let the Israelites go, Moses warned that God was about to send the worst hailstorm in Egypt's history. He told the Egyptians to get all their livestock and workers to shelter. Since they'd just had six mega-plagues, some Egyptians feared God and rushed their slaves and cattle indoors. Unfortunately, most Egyptians ignored Moses' warnings. *Not for long!* Suddenly God sent a deafening plague of baseball-sized hail. As it fell, lightning flashed back and forth. The hailstones beat down all the crops, stripped every tree, killed the cattle, and slew the slaves. (See Exodus 9:17–26.)

## Humongous Hailstones Hammer Helmets

The armies of five Amorite kings were camped around the city of Gibeon when Joshua and the Israelites attacked them. As the Amorite armies took off running down the road, the Israelites continued attacking them. As if *that* weren't bad enough, God rained down mongo hailstones that killed more Amorite soldiers than the Israelites had.

The Amorites hoped to hold out till sunset, but Joshua prayed for the sun to stand still, and for *one extra day* the sun didn't set! This was the Amorites' worst possible day . . . and it just refused to end! (See Joshua 10:5–14.)

## Never Heard Thunder *That* Loud!

Ever get scared by thunder? Once an army of macho, muscled warriors were spooked by super-loud rumbles. Samuel had called the Israelites together for a prayer meeting, and the Philistines thought, "Aha! Now let's wipe 'em out!" Samuel prayed and "the LORD thundered with loud thunder against the Philistines and threw them into . . . a panic." (See 1 Samuel 7:5–11.) No lightning. No hail. Just thunder. And Philistines peeling out. Must've been really L–O–U–D.

Q:
Why did Moses have such an easy time keeping his hair neat?

A:
Every time he lifted his hand to comb it, his hair parted.

## One Dust-Dry Drought Coming Up

King Ahab and Queen Jezebel were so wicked that Elijah said, "There will be neither dew nor rain in the next few years except at my word." The drought lasted *three years*. Then Elijah prayed for God to send rain, and a heavy rain came. Elijah calls for a drought? Got it! Then a gully washer? Got it! (See 1 Kings 17:1; 18:1–2, 41–45.) Next time you're tempted to laugh at the little old lady in your church praying for the weather or anything else . . . *don't!* She's onto something. You might want to join her. (See James 5:16–18.)

## Prophet Gets Slurped Up

This whirlwind dropped down, and its funnel had enough power to lift a 150-pound prophet right off the ground. It sucked Elijah into the air like a straw getting the last drops of a Slurpie. The younger prophets figured this was a regular tornado taxi—you know, the kind that picks up a cow in one pasture and drops it in another a few miles away—so they thought maybe Elijah had been dumped on some mountaintop. They looked and looked, but nope, he was up, up, and away to heaven. (See 2 Kings 2:1–18.)

## Sun Moves Backward! *Huh?*

Hezekiah was deathly sick from a boil, but when Isaiah told him God would heal him, Hez said if it was so, could God please give him a sign, like, oh, the shadow on the steps going *back* ten steps? (Hey, Hez! You want *the earth to stop rotating and go backward?*) Isaiah prayed and sure enough, the shadow went back up the steps. Then Isaiah mashed up some figs, plopped them down on the boil, and Hez was healed. (See 2 Kings 20:1–11.) Wow! God had to stop the world from spinning, just to convince Hez that mashed figs would suck the pus out of his boil?

## Rebuking the Wind and Waves

Jesus and his disciples were sailing across the Sea of Galilee when a furious storm came up and waves swept over the boat. His disciples freaked. "Yaaagggh! We're gonna drown!" Meanwhile Jesus was sprawled out on a fishnet, snoring away. He was completely soaked but sound asleep. The disciples shook him, wailing,

"Lord, save us!" Jesus yawned, got up, rebuked the wind and the waves, and . . . *dead calm.* Storm gone. (See Matthew 8:23–27.) Jesus said that a kingdom divided against itself couldn't stand (Matthew 12:25), so this wasn't a case of God sending a storm and Jesus stopping it. It was just some of that nasty weather caused by God's creation being mucked up by sin.

## Shutting Up the Sky

"Shutting up the sky" does not mean getting birds to stop singing. Revelation talks about two prophets who will have power to shut up the sky so it will not rain for three and a half years. Oh yeah, and while they're at it, they will have power to turn the waters into blood and to strike the earth with every kind of plague as often as they want. (See Revelation 11:6.) *As often as they want?* Hooo-eeee! That is power! The Bible talks about the gift of miracles (1 Corinthians 12:7–11). That's when God gives a ministry that involves miracles to someone—like Moses or Jesus, or these two prophets who have the gift of weather-control miracles.

## GET DEEPER

**Can you imagine** offering to make someone a cup of tea and the person saying, "Uh, I don't know if you can manage that. If you cook me a seven-course gourmet meal, *then* I'll believe you can boil water." That's kind of what Hezekiah did. "Hey, God. I'll know you can heal my boil if you can make time and the sun go backward." It sounds funny, but *we* do it with God, too. We know he can control weather and change world events, and we believe that he did all the huge miracles in the Bible, but we sometimes have trouble trusting him to take care of small things in our lives. Hey, God loves you and he's willing to hear and answer *all* your prayers—big and small. Talk to him now.

## Red Sea Splits

The Red Sea makes like a banana and splits! "All that night the Lord drove the sea back with a strong east wind and turned it into dry land. . . . The surging waters stood firm like a wall; the deep waters congealed" (Exodus 14:21; 15:8). People who try to come up with natural explanations to every miracle drive themselves crazy trying to figure out how this happened, but the simple fact is that it happened! When the waters "congealed," that means they became solid—like millions of tons of old Jell-O. They didn't turn into ice, but *some* very strange physics was at work on the water.

Some people try to say that the Israelites crossed through a very shallow part of the sea. It was like, oh, about two feet deep, and the water "parted" when the tide went out. Yeah? Well, how did the entire Egyptian army drown in two feet of water?

## Jordan River Dries Up

The Israelites crossed the Jordan River during the spring rains when the river had spilled over its banks into the flood plain, nearly a mile wide. It was, like, the *worst possible* time of year to try to cross. ("Um . . . whose idea was *this?* ") But as soon as the priests carrying the ark stepped into the river, the water level began dropping. Down, down, down it fell, till the riverbed was totally dry. The priests then stood with the ark in the middle of the riverbed for about twelve hours (sunrise to sunset) while three million people crossed. As soon as the Israelites had crossed and the priests carried the ark up out of the river bottom—*roaaaaarrr!*—the waters rushed downstream again. When the Canaanites heard of this miracle, "their hearts melted" like ice cream on a hot day. (See Joshua 3:14–17; 4:18; 5:1.)

## Swatting Jordan with a Cloak

One day Elijah and Elisha had to cross the Jordan River, so "Elijah took his cloak, rolled it up and struck the water with it. The water divided to the right and to the left, and the two of them crossed over on dry ground." Then Elijah was taken to heaven and Elisha had the cloak. How did he get back across the river? Simple. He struck the same river with the same cloak and it divided again. (See 2 Kings 2:8, 13–14.) It was about *time* people let that river know who was boss. Sure, Gortex can keep the rain off your back, but it can never repel water like Elijah's cloak did.

## Jonah's "Submarine Ride"

There's a terrific storm on the Mediterranean and Jonah knows it's because he disobeyed

God, so he says, "Chuck me overboard. I'll drown, sure, but God won't be upset anymore." *Ker-splash!* But God doesn't let Jonah off so easy. Some monster fish gulps him into its glop-filled gullet and away he goes on a submarine ride. If Jonah was scared of being trapped in a small place, this would've been the worst! And the *smell!* Finally, after Jonah repents, all the gut glop starts churning, the fish opens its mouth, and Jonah gets barfed onto the beach. (See Jonah 1–2.)

Teacher: Who knows a whale fact?

Girl: A whale swallowed the prophet Jonah.

Teacher: Impossible! Whales' throats can't swallow anything as big as a man.

Girl: I guess I'll ask Jonah about that when I get to heaven.

Teacher: Ha! And what if Jonah's in hell instead?

Girl: Then I guess you can ask him.

## Walking on Wild Waves

It's one thing to be on top of an epic wave on a surfboard. But imagine it *without* a board! No, we are not talking about bodysurfing. We are talking about *walking* on the waves. No way, you say?

Way! The waves weren't quite the size of ocean waves, since this was a big lake that was called a "sea." One night Jesus strolled out on the surging sea toward his disciples, who were in a boat. Peter thought he'd like to try that water-walking stuff, too. He actually did water-walk for some distance. *Cowabunga, dude!* Then he lost his nerve and down he went. Jesus had to drag him out of the water like a half-drowned cat. (See Matthew 14:22–33.) Pretty cool! Jesus not only walked on the water, but it held him up while he lifted a huge, heavy fisherman out of the sea.

## "Lost at Sea"—Wait! Maybe Not!

Paul and 275 people were on a ship sailing for Rome when a wind of hurricane force struck them. For fourteen days the storm raged. It was so dark, they couldn't see the sun. They finally lost all hope of being saved. They stopped eating too, because, like, what's the *use* of eating if you're just going to barf it over the rails? Paul was probably praying for God to stop the storm so they wouldn't sink or shipwreck, and God *did* a miracle, but it wasn't exactly what Paul had expected. It went like this: God told Paul the ship would wreck but that every single person would survive. And that's exactly what happened! (See Acts 27.) God has lots of ideas and he can perform a different kind of miracle each time.

GET COOLER

**When the Canaanites** heard about the Israelites' miraculous Jordan River crossing, their hearts melted. When Peter saw Jesus walk on the water, he was inspired to trust God and give it a try. When the sailors chucked Jonah overboard and the storm immediately stopped, they worshiped God. Probably many of the passengers God saved from the shipwreck—just as Paul said he would—became Christians. God answers our prayers not only to provide our needs and help us through seemingly impossible situations but because it shows people around us that he and his love are real.

## God Makes Contact

When the Israelites camped around Mount Sinai, "the LORD descended on it in fire" and "the whole mountain trembled violently." God wanted the Israelites to know that he was meeting with them on the mountain, so he gave it a little love tap. Later a psalmist compared Mount Sinai to a playful sheep. He joked, "Why was it . . . you mountains, that you skipped like rams?" (Psalm 114:5–6). The Israelites were freaked out. "Ah, Moses, God doesn't need to talk to us . . . No, really. Tell you what, you go and find out what he has to say and then you tell us. Please!" (See Exodus 19:16–19; 20:18–19.) It's funny how everyone is okay with God being "up there," but when he gets close "down here," everyone goes all weird.

## You've Gone Too Far!

Sometimes the earth splits open during an earthquake. One day a Levite named Korah led a rebellion against Moses and Aaron. "You have gone too far!" he insisted. "Why are *you* guys the leaders?" But Moses knew that the Levites were trying to snatch Aaron's job, and he answered, "You *Levites* have gone too far!" Next day, Moses told the people who lived near the tents of Korah, "Move back. If these men die naturally, then God didn't send me." Whooo-eee! Watch out! Korah and his gang of rebels didn't get a whole lot older. A second later "the ground under them split apart and the earth opened its mouth and swallowed them." (See Numbers 16:1–35.) Now then, anybody *else* want to argue with God's choice of leaders?

## Earthquakes with Meaning

Does God sometimes cause earthquakes? Yes. Isaiah 29:6 says, "The Lord Almighty will come with thunder and earthquake." When the nations fight against Jerusalem in the end days, the Lord will cause a huge earthquake: "The Mount of Olives will be split in two from east to west . . . with half of the mountain moving north and half moving south" (Zechariah 14:2–5). Maybe they'll call it the Mount of Sliced Olives after that.

God doesn't cause *all* earthquakes; most are just natural disasters caused by a sin-messed world. But when God wants to shake things up and get our attention, he can do it easily enough, and an earthquake is a good tool for the purpose. The instant Jesus died, God sent an earthquake to shake up the city and show his power. The earth shook, the rocks split, and the tombs broke open. The Roman soldiers were terrified! They said, "Surely he was the Son of God!" Again, when Jesus was raised from the dead, "there was a violent earthquake." (See Matthew 27:50–54; 28:1–2.) Scary stuff, and people got the point.

### God's Alarm Clock Wakes City

When Paul and Silas preached in Philippi, they were beaten, then chucked into prison. The officials who'd flogged them went home and tucked in for a good night's sleep. About midnight Paul and Silas were praising God when the heavenly alarm clock went off. "There was such a violent earthquake that the foundations of the prison were shaken. All the prison doors flew open, and everybody's chains came loose." The jailer woke up. Yeah, him . . . and everyone *else* in Philippi. He was so shaken up that he became a believer. (See Acts 16:16–34.)

### Get Deeper

**God used earthquakes** as one way to let people know that he was there and that he was working. When the rumbling began, the message was pretty clear. The Bible says that the Holy Spirit will lead Christians and guide us into all truth. As we get to know God better through prayer and his Word, we will experience his presence in our lives. God shouldn't have to shake our world to get our attention from the outside in. He can work quietly from the inside.

# NATURAL? OR SUPERNATURAL?

When the Bible describes a miracle, some people automatically wonder, "Was that supernatural or is there a natural explanation for it?" For example, when God dried up the flooded Jordan River so three million Israelites could cross—was that a supernatural miracle or was it just natural forces at work? Or both?

Joshua 3:16 says the Jordan River stopped flowing because "it piled up in a heap a great distance away, at a town called Adam." The cliffs are narrow at Adam, and sometimes landslides hit there and dam up the river. This happened in 1927; the Jordan was dammed up for more than twenty hours. Apparently, in Joshua's day the spring rains caused a landslide, the river dammed, the Israelites crossed, then—*ker-rrroaarr!*—the water broke the dam and rushed downriver again.

But even though there was a natural cause, it was still a miracle. Remember, the water cut off the *second* the priests stepped into the river. Talk about timing! God sent tons of rain at the exact right time to the exact right spot to cause the landslide at the exact same time he had millions of people in place to cross the Jordan.

On the other hand, God also parted the same river by a couple of totally *supernatural* miracles. Elijah struck the river with his cloak and—*fuwhoosh!*—it was as if a force field swept the water to the right and the left so he and Elisha could cross. An hour later Elisha did the same thing and again the water defied gravity—and probably about ten other natural laws—to let him pass. (See 2 Kings 2:8, 14.)

Remember when the Israelites moaned for meat, and the next day millions of quail came flopping down on their camp? Was that a supernatural miracle? No. If millions of *penguins* had tumbled out of the sky, *that* would have been a supernatural miracle. But quail normally do migrate over the Sinai Desert. All God had to do was tire them out with strong winds, then blow them a little to the west, a little to the east, then, "Israelite camp below! Incoming quail!" (See Numbers 11:31.) The timing of the birds' arrival was supernatural, however. It came as a direct response to Moses' prayer.

Professor: It really wasn't a miracle when the Israelites crossed the Red Sea. My calculations show that the water was only two feet deep in the spot.

Student: And the entire Egyptian army drowned in just two feet of water? That's even more of a miracle!

God can do anything and he can do it any way he wants to. Sometimes he does amazing things that defy or contradict natural laws. Sometimes he uses natural stuff like wind and rain to answer prayer. God is very creative and he always knows best. He may answer your prayers in big, unexplainable ways or in quiet, seemingly natural ways. It's still God at work and he just did something you couldn't do on your own. So either way it's a miracle.

## Three Million Slaves Set Free!

In Moses' day there were about three million Hebrew slaves in Egypt. God sent plague after plague to convince Pharaoh to set them free, but Pharaoh refused. He just didn't understand whom he was up against. It was a little like a three-year-old boy thinking he might win when wrestling a grown man. But God wasn't trying to impress Pharaoh. He was letting Israel and the world know that he was the one and only real God. Imagine a merchant who left Egypt when it still had all its slaves, coming back after the Exodus. He'd probably think the vanished slaves were a better trick than seeing an illusionist make a 747 disappear off the runway. "All right! Where are the mirrors?"

## Clear Out of Keilah!

David and his men already had enough trouble on their hands, hiding out in the wilderness to escape Saul's army. Then they heard that the Philistines were attacking the city of Keilah. David prayed, "Shall I go attack the Philistines?" The Lord said, "Yes." So David and his men risked their lives to save the city. ("Yeah, David! You're our hero!") Then David heard that Saul was coming to attack him, so he prayed, "Will the citizens of Keilah surrender me and my men to Saul?" The Lord said, "They will." ("Well, isn't *that* just great! Thanks, guys!") David then cleared out. Good thing God gave David a heads-up before Keilah give him a heads-off. (See 1 Samuel 23:1–13.) God led David supernaturally, like a chess coach giving a junior player all his moves,

David and his men were one move ahead of Saul and were never captured by Saul's army, no matter how hard the king tried.

### God Plays Hide-and-Seek

The prophet Jeremiah warned that God would judge Judah, and his friend Baruch read Jeremiah's prophecies to the king's officials. The officials said, "You and Jeremiah, go and hide. Don't let anyone know where you are." Sure enough, King Zedekiah sent men to arrest Jeremiah and Baruch. Did they find them? No. "The LORD had hidden them." (See Jeremiah 36:1–26.) The Bible doesn't say that Jeremiah found an especially good hiding place. It says, "The *LORD* had hidden them"—meaning that they could have been in an obvious place, but God blinded the officials' eyes, as when Jesus appeared to two of his disciples but "they were kept from recognizing him" (Luke 24:15–16).

Q:
What do Winnie the Pooh and John the Baptist have in common?

A:
Their middle name.

## Passing Through the Mob

Talk about touchy! Jesus preached a sermon to his old neighbors in the synagogue at Nazareth, and it made them so furious that they tried to throw him over a cliff. "But he walked right through the crowd and went on his way." (See Luke 4:16–30.) He didn't *fight* his way through dozens of angry bruisers. He *walked through.* Very likely, he did some kind of miracle so the mob either couldn't see him or couldn't stop him.

## Jailbirds Fly the Coop

Jesus had trained the twelve apostles to lead the church but Caiaphas, the high priest, chucked them in jail. If Caiaphas had killed them, that would have been a huge blow to God's plan. But that night an angel came along, unlocked the jail, and let the apostles out. The next morning, Caiaphas sent officers to bring the apostles to the Council meeting. The guards outside the prison cell opened the door and—to everyone's stunned amazement—the prison was empty! (See Acts 5:17–23.)

## Early Church Escape Artist

People must have thought that Paul was the greatest escape artist going. He escaped death as many times as Harry Houdini. One time a wild mob bashed him with bone-breaking boulders till he was dead—or so they *thought.* After they dumped his body outside the city gates—*get this!*—Paul got up and went back into the city. (See Acts 14:19–20.) Paul also survived three shipwrecks. He spent a night and a day hanging on to broken pieces of a ship. He was beaten with rods three different times, and *lived* after being whipped thirty-nine times on five different occasions. His back was whipped a total of 195 times! (See 2 Corinthians 11:24–25.)

## Tons More Miracles

As the writer of Hebrews said, "And what more shall I say?" We've run out of time to tell you about all the other heroes of faith "who through faith . . . shut the mouths of lions, quenched the fury of the flames . . ." (See Hebrews 11:32–34.) Hey! That's referring to Daniel in the lions' den and to his three friends Shadrach, Meshach, and Abednego surviving the fiery furnace! If you want to read about those amazing stories, see Daniel chapters 3 and 6.

GET STRONGER

Hebrews 11:32–35 talks about great men and women of God whose faith helped them accomplish miraculous things and survive seemingly impossible situations. Of course, it also talks about times when his people *weren't* miraculously rescued—and ended up being *killed* because they stood up for what they believed. Your life may never be threatened because of your faith, but whenever you find yourself in a tough spot, always do what is right and trust God. No matter what happens, you always come out ahead when you choose to please God and to trust him.

## WHEN BABIES ARE MIRACLES

With six billion people in the world, it'd seem that having babies is not a supernatural miracle. It's more of a natural event created by God. But some women simply *can't* bear children, and it takes a miracle for them to do so. This happened to several women in Bible times. Sometimes not only did they end up getting miracle babies, but those babies ended up doing great things for God.

## NURSERY GETS NOISE AGAIN

Abimelech, king of Gerar, had a wife and a whole slew of slave girls who got pregnant *all* the time. Suddenly all the women in his household couldn't have babies anymore. The royal nursery was getting really quiet. Why? Turns out Abraham and Sarah were visiting and Abim had snatched Sarah as yet *another* wife. It really seems strange, but God didn't let any of Abim's women have kids till he returned Sarah. Shortly after he did, the nursery started to fill up again. (See Genesis 20:1–18.)

## Ninety-Year-Old Mom

Abraham's wife, Sarah, was old enough to be a great-grandmother twenty times over, but she still hadn't had even *one* kid—and now she was *ninety!* So when God told Sarah she'd have a son, she laughed. Turns out the last laugh was on her. God performed a miracle and Sarah got pregnant and had a boy. Abraham (apparently in a funny mood) named the kid Isaac. That's Hebrew for "laughter." (See Genesis 18:1–15; 21:1–7.) If they'd had a girl, what would he have named her? Giggles?

## Bawling Baby by Bulrushes

Pharaoh had a law that all Hebrew baby boys had to be thrown into the Nile River. When Moses was born, his mom hid him as long as she could, but when he became too big—and loud—she put him in a basket and set him among the reeds. Soon Pharaoh's daughter came down to take a bath and found the basket. She knew Moses was Hebrew, but instead of chucking him to the crocs, she adopted him! Suddenly Moses' sister stepped out and asked Pharaoh's daughter if she wanted a nanny to look after him. She did, so Sis ran to get her mother, and Moses' own mom kept him until he was old enough to live in the palace. Talk about a sweet miracle. A praying mom went from hiding her baby from soldiers to getting paid to watch her own son, and all under a "royal decree." (See Exodus 1:22–2:10.)

## Angel Rolls Out Welcome Wagon

In some cities, the Welcome Wagon people come by with gifts when a mom has a baby. One time in Israel the angel of the Lord showed up about a year *before* the baby was born to tell Manoah and his wife they'd *have* a baby.

"Oh yeah, and your kid will be super-special. He'll start delivering Israel from the Philistines."

"Hey, thanks! That's better than a hundred-dollar gift certificate."

Sure enough, the woman gave birth to a boy, and they named him Samson. (See Judges 13.) Yup, you heard right: *Samson.* Makes you wonder if Samson's dad had trouble play-wrestling with his three-year-old son. "Okay, Samson dear, it's time for dinner. Let Daddy get up."

## High Priest Blunders, Then Blesses

Was the high priest's face ever red! Eli was sitting by the temple door, watching people pray, when he noticed a lady's lips moving silently. He yelled, "How long will you keep on getting drunk? Get rid of your wine." Oops. Turns out the lady was a well-respected citizen of Ramathaim who couldn't have kids. She was praying for a miracle baby. Well then, Eli blessed her, saying, "May the God of Israel grant you what you have asked of him." Well, God did. Shortly after that Hannah had a son. (See 1 Samuel 1:1–20.) His name was Samuel and he was one of the greatest men of God in the Bible.

## King Bone-Burner's Coming

Talk about planning ahead! God announced the birth of a baby named Josiah hundreds of years ahead of time. When Israel divided into the kingdom of Judah in the south and the kingdom of Israel in the north, the northern king,

Jeroboam, turned away from God. He appointed pagan priests to sacrifice to an idol at the altar in Bethel. A man of God prophesied that one day a king of Judah named Josiah would kill the pagan priests, and to show how much God hated the idol's altar, he would burn human bones on it. *Three hundred years later,* King Amon had a son and named him Josiah. Josiah loved God with all his heart and did exactly what the prophet said he would do and burned the bones of pagan priests. (See 1 Kings 13:1–3; 2 Kings 23:15–20.)

## Before Jerry Was Born

God told the prophet Jeremiah, "Before I formed you in the womb I knew you." God also said, "Before you were born . . . I appointed you as a prophet." Before Jeremiah's mom was even pregnant, God knew Jeremiah would be coming along; then he formed Jeremiah in the womb—made him who he was—and appointed him as a prophet. (See Jeremiah 1:4–5.) Wow! A question we should all be asking is not "What do I want to be when I grow up?" but "What is God's plan for me when I grow up?"

## God Predicts, Picks King

Over one hundred years before Cyrus was born, God mentioned him *by name.* And 150 years before Cyrus did a single thing, God said he would:

a. defeat Babylon

b. let the Jews return to Judea

c. give the order to rebuild Jerusalem

d. rebuild the temple

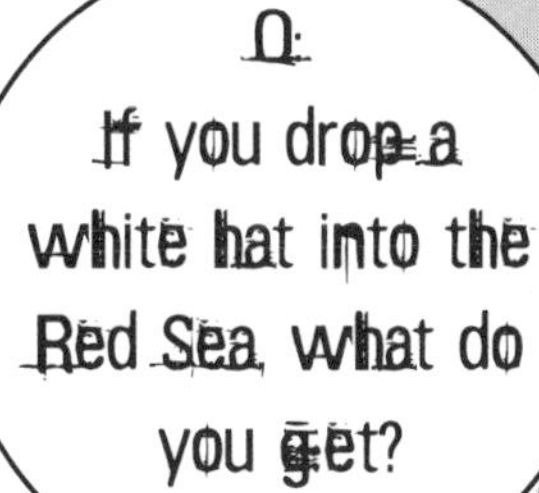


Why did God plan this? He said, "So that you may know that I am the LORD, the God of Israel, who summons you *by name.*" Whew! Talk about being in charge of history! (See Isaiah 44:24–45:4, 13.)

## Gobs of Miracles for John

John the Baptist was a miracle baby!

Miracle 1: God picked as his parents a couple too old to have kids.

Miracle 2: An angel showed up to announce John's birth.

Miracle 3: The angel struck Dad dumb because he doubted.

Miracle 4: God predicted that John would be like Elijah and prepare the way for the Lord. He did.

Miracle 5: John was filled with the Holy Spirit before he was even born.

Miracle 6: After John was born, his dad could suddenly talk again.

No wonder all the neighbors said, "Wow! What is *this* child going to be?" (See Luke 1:5–25, 57,66.)

**It was cool** when God knew what someone's name would be and what he or she would do, long before that person was even born! It's really cool when God chooses people to do special tasks that only they can do! Guess what? This applies to you too. God knew everything about you, including when you'd be born. Even though you may have your dad's nose and your mom's eyes, it was God who created your spirit and made you who you are. Not only that, but he knew what he wanted you to do, even before he made you and gave you the talents, abilities, and desires to match. David wrote about this in Psalm 139. You are special to God and he has a plan just for you. Pray and tell him that you want to follow his plan every day of your life.

GET DEEPER

When Moses ran from Egypt to Midian, he turned in his prince's scepter for a shepherd's staff. He picked a sapling tree—nothing special—chopped it down, and instant staff! Beware! Moses is armed and dangerous. No kidding. That stick became known as the staff of God, and it was used to perform more miracles than any other piece of wood in the Bible.

First time we see the staff is at the burning bush when God says Moses will deliver the Hebrews from Egypt. Moses needs a sign, so God says, "What is that in your hand?"

Moses says, "A staff."

God says, "Throw it down."

Moses throws it down. *Whaaaaaa!* It turns into a snake—like a six-foot-long Egyptian cobra. Moses runs.

God says, "Take it by the tail." (Not

he head. The *tail*. That thing could whip around and bite in an instant.)

Moses does and it stiffens into a staff. "Cool. But will it go cobra when I set it down tonight?"

Then God says, "Take this staff in your hand so you can perform miraculous signs with it."

When Moses gets to Egypt, he hands the staff to Aaron. Aaron throws it down and it goes all snakey for the elders, then back to wood. They believe. He throws it down in front of Pharaoh and it's cobra time again! Pharaoh's magicians say, "Big deal," and their staffs morph into snakes, too. Yeah. But then God's snake *eats* their snakes—talk about stuffed—then stiffens back into a stick.

Pharaoh refuses to listen, so Aaron raises the staff and strikes the Nile River. *Whack!* River turns into blood. Pharaoh hardens his

heart, so God has them stretch out the staff again: a plague of frogs comes, then swarms of gnats and flies, then a plague on livestock, then a plague of boils, then a killer hailstorm, then a locust plague, and finally weird darkness. (See Exodus 3–10.)

The next time we see the staff, Moses is raising it over the Red Sea. *Whoooo-ooossssssh!* The Red Sea parts. When the Egyptian army tries to follow the Hebrews across, Moses stretches out ol' Staffy, and—*kerrr-raaassssssh!*—millions of tons of water crash down on the Egyptians. (See Exodus 14:15–28.)

Wonder Wood is back in action when the Israelites are in the dry desert. Moses uses the staff to whack a rock and out spurts water. A short while later the Amalekites attack the Israelites, and the Israelites *only* win the battle because Moses manages, with a little help from his friends, to hold the staff over his head until the battle is finished. (See Exodus 17:1–13.)

Two years later the staff comes back to life again, not as a snake but as an almond tree. Cool! It bears buds, flowers, and even almond nuts. God uses it as a sign that he has chosen Aaron to be high priest. The other guys who want the job can't get their staffs to produce nuts or nuttin'. Moses then takes this most incredible staff out of circulation and stores it in front of the ark of the covenant. (See Numbers 17:1–10.)

Nearly forty years later the Israelites are desperate for water again, so God tells Moses to bring the staff back out and speak to the rock. Moses figures, "Hey, I'm holding the staff. Why not *use* it?" So he smacks the rock. Twice. Sure, water comes out, but the rod was just supposed to *be* there, not get *used.* (See Numbers 20:2–12.)

Later on, the staff is placed *inside* the ark (Hebrews 9:3–4). Hmmm . . . wonder how it *fit* in there? The ark was only three feet long (Exodus 25:10) and, uh, the staff was about *six* feet long. You don't suppose that Moses *broke it in half* when he beat the rock?

Within a few hundred years the staff of God has vanished (1 Kings 8:9). What happened? No one knows. But it makes you wonder where the idea came from for all the stories about wizards with magical staffs. The difference is of course that Moses wasn't a wizard and his staff wasn't magic. God merely used it as a prop. It was God who did all the miracles.

## ONE SERIOUSLY SICK PHARAOH

Getting sick can be a miracle, though maybe not the kind of miracle you want. When the pharaoh of Egypt decided to add Abraham's wife, Sarah, to his harem, he ended up with a personal palace plague as an unexpected bonus. "The LORD inflicted serious diseases on Pharaoh and his household." This is not like getting the measles. We are talking *serious* diseases. Pharaoh promptly gave Sarah back to Abraham and sent him away. (See Genesis 12:14–20.) The Bible doesn't say that God cured Pharaoh after that, but he probably did.

## MOSES GETS PART-TIME LEPROSY

One time God gave Moses instant leprosy, but (fortunately for Moses) it nstantly disappeared. God ntended it to be a sign. Moses put his hand inside nis robe, and when he orought it out, it was leprous. Then he put it back and took it out and it was fine again. (See Exodus 4:6–7, 29–31.) Having his wooden staff turn to a snake already freaked out Moses enough. Can you imagine how he felt when he saw his hand full of disease, his flesh rotten and almost falling off? He probably hoped that God would use the stick sign more often than the diseased-hand sign.

## SRAELITE SNOW WHITE

Miriam disapproved of Moses' marriage to a Cushite woman, but Moses had the final say. He *was* God's prophet, after all. Miriam thought, *Hey, I'm a prophet, too! Moses should*

*listen to me!* God didn't think so and he instantly turned Miriam into a snow-white leper, her flesh half-eaten away. It was *not* a pretty sight. Aaron begged Moses to ask God to heal her. God did, uh huh, but he gave her seven days as a leper to think about things first. (See Numbers 12.) That ended Miriam's career as a marriage counselor.

## The Shrivel-Up Miracle

When a prophet showed up in Bethel and spoke against idolatry, wicked King Jeroboam stretched out his hand and said, "Seize him!" Instantly his hand shriveled up. Suddenly none of the guards were eager to reach out and seize the prophet. It *juuuust* didn't seem like a good idea. (See 1 Kings 13:1–6.)

## You Should've Asked *God*

King Ahaziah's upper room had a balcony surrounded by a wood lattice covered with grapevines. Great place to enjoy the view and pop grapes in your mou—*whoaaaah!* Ahaziah leaned a little too hard, broke through the lattice, and injured himself big-time. He *might* have recovered if he hadn't sent a messenger to Baal-Zebub, god of Ekron, to ask, "Will I recover?" God had Elijah shortstop the king's messenger and basically tell him, "Just for consulting a false prophet, you die." (See 2 Kings 1:2–6.) God didn't take kindly to the king of Israel leading his people into idolatry.

## Gehazi Gets Naaman's Leprosy

After God healed a foreign general, Naaman, of leprosy, Elisha refused to accept any reward. (He didn't want Naaman to think he could pay God to heal him. Besides, Elisha was just the messenger; God had done the healing.) But Elisha's servant, greedy Gehazi, ran after Naaman, made up a story, scored some loot, then stashed it, thinking that Elisha would never know. Not too smart. God sees everything and Elisha was a prophet. So when Gehazi returned, Elisha said, "Is this the time to take money? . . . Naaman's leprosy will cling to you and to your descendants forever." Gehazi stumbled away as white as snow. (See 2 Kings 5.)

## And Now . . . Forehead Leprosy

Leprosy was *the* big bad disease to not get back in Bible days, and if you got it, you couldn't hang out with other people. You definitely could not enter God's temple. Well, one day proud King Uzziah decided he was "spiritual" enough to go into the temple and do a job only priests were allowed to do. When the priests stopped him, Uzziah threw a fit. "Don't you know I'm the king? I could have your heads for—"

Suddenly leprosy broke out on Uzziah's forehead. He had leprosy the rest of his life. He had to live alone and couldn't go into the temple ever again. (See 2 Chronicles 26:16–21.)

Q: You've heard the expression, "shadow of a doubt." Who had a shadow of faith?

A: Peter. People believed that if his shadow fell on them, they'd be healed of their diseases (Acts 5:15).

GET COOLER

One of the biggest lies the Devil has ever circulated is, "Do whatever you want as long as you're not hurting anyone else." But doing things God's way is the only way that works. Doing things any other way always hurts us and others. In the Bible there are many stories of God judging people and even ending their lives because what they were doing would have hurt others and led many more into being like them. The two greatest commandments are to love God and to love others. Doing wrong hurts others, so God knows that when we do things our way and disobey him, we aren't loving him or others. Even just setting a wrong example hurts those watching us. Plus if we're doing wrong, the good things that we *could* be doing aren't happening. The stories about leprosy show this message: leprosy was contagious, just as disobedience to God is. Our example affects others.

## Snakey Cure for Snakebite

Talk about weird! In the desert the Israelites were telling God things like, "Why did you bring us here to die?" and "We detest this miserable manna!" They were grumbling and complaining to God big-time! Suddenly swarms of venomous snakes slithered into camp, biting everyone in sight. When the Israelites said they were sorry, God told Moses to make a bronze snake and put it on a pole. *Hammer, hammer, beat, wham!* "Hurry, Moses! That snake doesn't have to be perfect!" The snake went up and anyone who had been bitten looked at it and lived. (See Numbers 21:4–9.)

# General Becomes the Big Dipper

Poor Naaman! He's the rich and powerful head of the Aramean army but he has leprosy. He needs a miracle. So he gets in his chariot and rides all the way to Israel to ask the God of the Israelites to heal him. *Screech!* Chariot stops at Elisha's house. Naaman expects Elisha to come out, get all excited about how important Naaman is, and do some fancy healing ceremony for celebrities. Elisha doesn't even show. He sends a messenger who says, "Go, wash yourself seven times in the Jordan." What? No special ceremony? No Elisha . . . just his servant?

When Naaman finally swallows his pride and says, "Oh, all right then," and takes one, two, three, four, five, six, seven dips, his flesh is completely healed!

(See 2 Kings 5:1–14.) God wanted Naaman to know that he was healing him not because he was important but simply because he asked and believed.

## The Centurion's Sick Servant

When the servant of a Roman centurion was paralyzed and suffering, the centurion went out, found Jesus, and asked him to heal his servant. Jesus started walking toward the centurion's house but the man said, "Just say the word, and my servant will be healed." When Jesus heard this, he was astonished. This Roman had more faith than anyone in the land of Israel. *Was* his servant healed? You bet! The centurion went home and found out that his servant had started getting better at the same time that he'd been talking to Jesus. (See Matthew 8:5–13.)

Q:
What did Balaam's donkey say after he beat her with a stick?

A:
Beats me (Numbers 22:23–33).

## Sorry, the Cook Is Sick

Peter took Jesus home for dinner one night. He probably told him, "You gotta taste my mother-in-law's roast lamb! She's the best cook in Capernaum!" But when they got there, Mom was sick with a fever. Fever schmever. Jesus touched her hand and she was healed. She got up and began to wait on him. (See Matthew 8:14–15.)

## If It's No Bother

One day a man with leprosy begged Jesus, "If you are willing, you can make me clean." The guy didn't even question whether Jesus *could* do the miracle. He knew he could. He just hoped Jesus was willing. And he was. Jesus touched him and he was cured. (See Mark 1:40–45.)

## Rip Open the Roof!

Four guys hear that Jesus is inside a house in their neighborhood, so they carry a paralyzed friend there on a mat. Problem: the crowd is so thick around the house, they can't even get near the door. You gotta hand it to these guys. Instead of giving up, they climb onto the flat roof and begin digging through.

Jesus is teaching below when all this clay and dust start raining on people's heads. Next thing you know, a man on a mat is lowered through a hole in the roof and lands on the floor. Four dusty faces look down. "Think you could heal

him?" Jesus does. (See Mark 2:1–12.) The Bible says that Jesus saw their faith. How do you *see* faith? If people believe something, they *act* upon it. The men believed so intensely that Jesus would heal their friend, they were ready to do anything to get him to Jesus.

## SHOUTING IN SAMARIA

Ten men from a leper colony on the Galilee-Samaria border saw Jesus entering a village. Since they weren't allowed to come near the village, they stood at a distance and shouted, "JEEEEESUS, MASTER, HAVE PIIIIITY ON US!" With ten of them shouting, they had a pretty good echo going. Jesus had a good set of lungs, so he shouted back, "GO, SHOW YOURSELVES TO THE PRIIEEEESTS!" (That was what lepers were supposed to do if they thought they were healed.) As they went, they were healed. One guy ran back, threw himself at Jesus' feet, and thanked him. (See Luke 17:11–19.) Hey! What happened to the other nine? Were they planning on mailing thank-you cards? When God does something for us, we should say, "Thank you." Ten men were healed but only one got close to Jesus.

## Wow! The Exact Same Time!

When Jesus arrived in Cana after a long walk from Judea, he met a royal official whose son was deathly sick in Capernaum, twenty miles away. The official asked Jesus to come heal his son. Instead Jesus said, "You may go. Your son will live." So the man went.

The next day his servants met him on the road with the good news: "Your son is healed!"

"When?"

"Yesterday at the seventh hour."

"Wow! That's the *exact time* Jesus said so!" (See John 4:43–53.)

## Unauthorized Tap into Miracle Power

Jesus was in the middle of a crowd and it was like a New York subway at rush hour, with people pushing and shoving and practically crushing Jesus. Suddenly Jesus asked, "Who touched me?" ("Well, like, *dozens* of people, Lord.") Turns out a lady with a bleeding disorder had touched the edge of Jesus' robe and

siphoned off some miracle power. Jesus felt the power leave his body. The lady 'fessed up and said, "I'm healed." (See Luke 8:40–48.) She had thought, *If I could just touch the hem of his garment, I'd be healed.* And that's what happened.

## No More of This!

When Jesus was arrested, Peter decided to "protect" him, so—*slliisshh!*—he drew a sword, took a swing at a dude named Malchus, and hacked off his right ear. Now, "Milk-us" sounds like a cow's name, but *anyway*, blood started spurting out and his ear dropped into the bushes. Jesus said, "No more of this!" Someone picked up the ear and handed it to Jesus. Then Jesus just touched Malchus's ear. Malchus was howling in pain, blood running all over his face and arm. Suddenly his ear was stuck back on and the pain was gone. It all happened so fast, his head was spinning. (See Luke 22:47–51; John 18:10.)

Q:
How many times did Jesus use his spit to heal people?

A:
Three times (See Mark 7:33; 8:23; John 9:6).

## Crippled Man Jumps!

One day this poor crippled guy was sitting in the temple gate begging. When he asked Peter and John for money, Peter said, "In the name of Jesus the Messiah of Nazareth, *walk!*" Peter grabbed his hand, pulled him up, and immediately the man began walking and jumping. Now, miracle number one was that his legs were made whole. Miracle two was that the guy was over forty years old and had *never walked!* Bet some of his jumps were pretty wild. Five thousand people saw him jumping and became Christians. (See Acts 3:1–4:4.)

## Standing in the Light

Sometimes when you stand between your sister and the light, she complains, "Hey, you're in my light!" No one complained when the apostle Peter did that. Word got out that Peter had the power to heal, so people wanted to touch him. Problem was, they didn't always know where to find him. They *did* know that he walked to the temple every day, so they laid sick folks on the sides of the street so when Peter walked by, his *shadow* would fall on them and heal them. And it did! Now, Peter's shadow was not miraculous, but Peter had healing power and when people reached out in faith, God honored it. (See Acts 5:12–16.)

## Take Away the Bulls!

In Lystra Paul and Barnabas met another man who had been lame from birth. Paul said, "Stand up on your feet!" and again the man jumped up and began to walk. The crowds were so blown away that they thought Paul and Barnabas were gods. They brought bulls to sacrifice to them. (See Acts 14:8–18.) Now, *that* was weird.

## Not One Sick Person on Malta

Publius, chief official of the island of Malta, was already having problems: his father was confined to bed with fever and dysentery. To make matters worse, this morning a ship with 276 passengers wrecked on the beach below his estate. Or was that a *good* thing? Publius thought so! One of the castaways, Paul, had just been bitten by a viper but survived. Paul then placed his hands on Publius's dad and healed him! After this every sick person on the island showed up and was cured. (See Acts 28:1–9.)

**It's funny, but** some Bible stories tell about people who disobeyed God and got sick; others tell of people who followed God but got sick; some tell about those who disobeyed God and didn't get sick. On the healing side, God healed his people and sometimes healed his people's enemies. We don't have to understand how all this works, but we do know that sickness is in the world because it's a fallen, imperfect place. In heaven there won't be any sickness or suffering. Just because someone is sick—like the man born blind—doesn't mean that God is "judging him" or that it's God's will that he be that way. The Bible says we should pray for the sick and trust that God hears and answers our prayers. God made our bodies and wants us to be healthy and strong (3 John 2). And remember, a big part of being healthy is looking after your body.

GET STRONGER

Some people have no idea what a miracle is. They've heard that when you pray, God answers in his own way and in his own time. But the idea of God being in charge bugs them. They want it to be like flicking on a light switch. Snap your fingers and it appears. Wave a wand and it materializes.

But God is not like some imaginary genie in a bottle, or a magical "force" that you can call to your aid. He is our heavenly Father and he wants us to grow and become more like Jesus. He also wants us to have a relationship with him. God can perform miracles and answer prayer, but he also knows that, for example, if we pray for a million dollars, we won't learn much or become better Christians if he gives it to us.

A lot of people wish they had "magical powers" and could just make things happen. You know, load themselves down with goodies and make bad things happen to their enemies. But God knows that would be harmful to us and to others. God keeps control of his power for our own good. He's the only one with the wisdom and knowledge to always use it for everyone's good.

Once a guy called Simon practiced sorcery and amazed people with his magical tricks. But he was astonished when he saw Philip doing *greater* signs and miracles. When he saw Peter and John pray for people to receive the power of God's Spirit, Simon thought they did it by magic. He offered them money to give him that "magical power." Peter gave Simon such a stiff rebuke that Simon groveled for mercy. (See Acts 8:9–24.) Simon didn't understand how God works; he thought Peter and John were the

ones with the power, and he wanted to have it. But he didn't want it to help others and do God's will. He wanted it for selfish reasons. That's why Peter told him off.

Later Paul met a sorcerer named Bar-Jesus. He called himself Elymas—a fancy way of saying "Sorcerer." When Paul was telling a Roman governor about Jesus, Elymas tried to stop the governor from believing. Paul looked Elymas in the eye and said, "You are a child of the devil. . . . Now the hand of the Lord is against you. You are going to be blind . . . for a time." And it was lights-out—*instantly.* (See Acts 13:4–12.)

We don't know how God's power works or how supernatural powers and forces of the universe work. God doesn't show us that in his Word. But Paul called Elymas a child of the Devil because he was an enemy of the gospel. He wanted power so he could have what he wanted, without learning, growing, or submitting to God.

In Moses' day the magicians imitated some of the signs and miracles Moses did, and the Bible talks about witchcraft, divination, astrology, and other ways of fooling around with supernatural power instead of submitting to God. God tells us to stay away from all that stuff because it takes away from his love and his plan for us. They are selfish, harmful attempts to take shortcuts in life.

All the occult together doesn't have the power that God has in his little finger. God can do anything. He's our Father and he wants to do wonderful things in our lives, but we need to trust him. He knows when to perform huge miracles and when to teach us to be better Christians. Hey, miracles rule, magic drools!

Q:
The Bible tells us that Methuselah lived to be 969 years. Other men lived to be 910 years (Genesis 5:14, 27). Why doesn't it say how old the oldest women were?

A:
They wouldn't tell their age.

## A Demon-Possessed Town?

Mark 1:32–33 says, "The people brought to Jesus all the sick and demon-possessed. The whole town gathered at the door." This does *not* mean that the whole town was demon-possessed. Some of the townspeople were simply sick, some of them brought the sick, and everyone else was there to see God's power in action. They weren't disappointed.

## Seven Demons Down and Out

Some people think seven is God's perfect number. But it isn't always. Just ask Mary Magdalene. We don't know who was counting, but when she came to Jesus, he cast seven demons out of her. (See Luke 8:2.)

## Naked Chain-Snapping Guy

The chain-breaking streaker lost his power when Jesus drove hundreds of demons out of him. This poor guy was living naked among the tombstones, cutting himself with rocks and howling like a werewolf. He had often been chained, but he kept snapping the chains, and after a while the people ran out of chains *and* out of guys willing to sneak up on him to chain him. But when Jesus came along, one word and the demons begged for mercy, packed their bags, and rushed into a low-rent neighborhood—a herd of pigs. (See Mark 5:1–13.) Even the pigs couldn't stand the company, so they ran off a cliff into the water and drowned.

## Into the Water, into the Fire, out of the Kid

A vicious demon once possessed a young boy and constantly threw him into the water or the fire, trying to kill him. When Jesus showed up, the boy fell to the ground and rolled around, foaming at the mouth. Gross! Jesus commanded the demon to leave and the spirit shrieked, convulsed the boy violently, and came out. Problem was, the boy looked so much like a corpse that people thought he'd died. ("Umm, killing him was *not* what we had in mind, Lord.") Relax. The boy was still alive. Jesus helped him to his feet. (See Mark 9:14–29.)

## Python, Begone!

One time Paul met a girl who had a spirit that let her predict the future. The Greeks called this the "python" spirit. They thought the mythical snake of Delphi spoke through people. (Gives you the willies, huh?) Anyway, when this fortune-teller began to pester Paul, he said, "In the name of Jesus Christ I command you to come out of her!" And the evil spirit split! Gone! (See Acts 16:16–19.) The people who had been making money from her fortune-telling weren't very happy—but the woman was free!

GET DEEPER

**When Jesus was** on the earth, he had no trouble taking control over demons. They knew who he was and were shaking in their boots (or whatever they wear on their feet). Paul also had no problem. He wrote that the name of Jesus is the name above all names and that every being above earth, in the earth, and below the earth must bow to that name. Jesus gave the church the authority to do things in his name, so demons still quake in their boots when Christians use the name of Jesus.

## Mediterranean Seaside Miracle

One time Elijah was staying with a widow and her son in the seaside city of Zarephath. His upper room had a view, too. Seagulls. Salt air. Cool. But one day the widow's son got so sick, he stopped breathing. The widow was all torn up. So Elijah took the boy up to his room and prayed, "O LORD my God, let this boy's life return to him!" And suddenly the boy rose from the dead! (See 1 Kings 17:7–9, 17–24.) Now, *that* would be a vacation to remember!

## Sunstruck Son

Here's a healing miracle from Shunem and a reminder to stay out of the sun. It was a scorcher out there one day, and a boy was in the fields with his father, watching the reapers, when he complained of head pains. He had severe sunstroke and by noon he was dead. Instead of mourning him, the boy's mother took off riding, found the prophet Elisha, and brought him back. When Elisha arrived at her home, he prayed for the boy, and—miracle of miracles!—the boy was raised from the dead. (See 2 Kings 4:8–37.)

## Prophet's Bones Zap Corpse!

Elisha died and was buried. Later some Israelites were burying a man and saw a band of Moabite raiders riding up. "Run for your lives!" They chucked the corpse into Elisha's tomb and took off. The instant the dead man hit Elisha's bones—probably knocking them all over the place—he came back to life. (See 2 Kings 13:20–21.) Can't you just see the Moabite raiders

riding up as this mummy comes walking out of the tomb? *Whoo-ooo-oooooo!* Must've totally spooked them!

## Conversation in a Coffin

Once Jesus and his disciples approached the town of Nain, and "a large crowd" was with them. They met a funeral procession coming out and it was "a large crowd," too. Whew! Large crowd meets large crowd. Jesus felt so sorry for the dead boy's mother that he went up and touched the coffin. Jesus said, "Young man . . . get up!" He didn't say, "*And* start talking," but that's what the boy did. (See Luke 7:11–17.) The men carrying his coffin were probably so startled that they just about dropped him.

In 2 Kings 2:11 the horses of heaven are described as "horses of fire"!

Can you imagine catching one of them and trying to put a saddle on it? It would burn to ashes!

## Keep the Money, Just Be Quiet

In Jesus' day, when someone died the family mourned loudly and publicly. If you were wealthy like Jairus, you could hire professional mourners to help wail and make a noise.

These were women who cried for a living. (Hey, today they work in Hollywood.) When Jesus came to Jairus' house, he told the crowd, "Stop wailing. Go away. The girl is not dead but asleep." The mourners kept at it. They knew she was dead. Besides, they'd been *paid* to mourn and they were gonna mourn. Jesus shut them all out of the house and prayed for the girl to come back to life. And she *did!* Jesus not only shut the mourners out; he shut them up. Kind of hard to mourn if no one's dead. (See Matthew 9:18–26; Luke 8:40–42, 49–55.) Wonder if they still got paid?

## Four Days Dead and Stinky

It's one thing to raise someone from the dead when they've just been dead for a few hours or a day. They're stiff and pale but they haven't rotted yet. What if they've, like, been dead for days and smell higher than your older brother's stinky gym socks? When Jesus showed up at Lazarus' tomb, he said, "Take away the stone." Laz's sister Martha wasn't sure she *wanted* to. He'd been dead for four days. "But, Lord, by this time there is a bad odor." Jesus wasn't fazed. When the stone was moved, he shouted, "Lazarus, come out!" and Laz came walking out, wrapped up like a mummy! (See John 11:1–44.)

## Results of the Joppa-Lydda Run

The entire town of Joppa was astonished! A couple days previously a Christian lady named Tabitha had died. She was well known and well loved. While some friends prepared to bury her, two guys—who hoped that God might have other plans—broke all records in a run to a nearby town, where they found the apostle Peter. When Peter showed up in Joppa, he prayed, then said, "Tabitha, get up." It was majorly weird when the dead woman opened her eyes, but half the town became believers! (See Acts 9:36–42.)

Today businesspeople talk about "power dressing." Jesus was truly a power dresser! A woman touched the edge of his cloak and power left Jesus and healed her.

## As I Was Saying . . .

One time Paul was in Troas meeting with fellow Christians, and he kept talking till midnight. A kid named Eutychus was sitting in the window three stories up, and as Paul went on and on, he fell asleep. Next thing you know, *"Yaaggghh!"* then *whummp!* Euty was dead. But Paul prayed and the next thing you know,

The story spread and crowds scrambled to touch his clothes (Mark 5:34–30; Matthew 14:35–36).

he was alive again. Everyone went back upstairs and Paul continued talking till daylight. (See Acts 20:6–12.) You *awake* there, Eutychus? (That was probably the last time he fell asleep in church!)

## A Question for Agrippa

Raising dead people back to life is a huge miracle. But like the apostle Paul asked King Agrippa, "Why should any of you consider it incredible that God raises the dead?" (Acts 26:8). Yeah. Good question. Why should you? God is all-powerful. Raising the dead is no big deal for him. So get a grip, Agrippa.

## Party's Over, Boys

The book of Revelation talks about two prophets who will bring plagues on the earth for three and a half years. Then the Antichrist will kill them and leave their bodies to rot on Main Street. People will be so happy that they'll be celebrating and sending gifts to each other. ("Oh, look what I got! A nose plug! Those guys are starting to smell!") But the party will shut down after a few days when the prophets come back to life, stand up, then rise to heaven. (See Revelation 11:3–12.) Imagine seeing that one on CNN!

Every time God raised someone from the dead, it got people's attention big-time. Everyone knows that only God can do that. There's another kind of "raising from the dead" that gets people's attention, though: when we become Christians, we go from being dead spiritually because of sin to becoming alive spiritually because of what Jesus did. We become different people, changed on the inside—God's children. When we tell others about how that happened to us, it's powerful and gets their attention. The Bible says that we overcome by the blood of the Lamb and by the word of our testimony (Revelation 12:11). That's the gospel story combined with how it changed us. Telling people what God has done and is doing in your life can help raise another lost soul from the dead.

GET COOLER

## Name and Job Description

Several times God named people and described what they'd do in life—many years before they were born. He did that with Josiah, Cyrus, and John the Baptist. He *really* went to town when it came to his own Son, Jesus Christ. Hundreds and thousands of years before Jesus was born, the Bible made dozens of promises that a Savior (Messiah) would come, who would be the Son of God. Many Bible prophecies spelled out the details of the Messiah's birth, life, death, and resurrection. They even named the town he would be born in.

For the Messiah to be God's Son, God had to be his Father. *Literally*. He couldn't just have a normal, hairy-chested dad. That's why Isaiah prophesied, "The virgin will be with child and will give birth to a son, and they will call him . . . God with us"

(Matthew 1:23; Isaiah 7:14). The Messiah's mom had to have a son without ever having had sex with a man. That would be a miracle. Sure enough, God's Spirit came over Mary and caused her to become pregnant with Jesus (Matthew 1:18–25).

## Back from the Dead—Forever!

Everybody dies. A few people died and came back, finished living, then died for good. But no one ever came back in a body that would live *forever.* Only Jesus did that. He had been dead a few days, but early Sunday morning the Holy Spirit raised his corpse back to life! In fact, God completely transformed his body into a supernatural body. This shocked Jesus' friends, family, and enemies. No one was expecting that! Yet it had been prophesied in the Bible hundreds of years earlier.

(See Luke 24:13–27; Acts 2:22–32.) If you visit Jesus' tomb today in Israel, you'll find it quite different from the graves of other famous people. It's unoccupied . . . empty! Jesus didn't really need a tomb. He just needed to borrow one for a few days while he paid the price for our sins.

### Post-Resurrection Powers

Even before he was raised from the dead, Jesus had power to stop a storm and defy gravity by walking on water (Mark 4:35–39; 6:47–48). Once he was raised from the dead and had a glorious, eternal body, he could *really* rock. He could appear and disappear at will (Luke 24:30–31), pass through locked doors (John 20:19), float straight up through the air (Luke 24:50–51), and blind those who looked on him (Acts 9:3–5, 8).

### Jesus Gets His Glory Back!

Jesus once prayed to his Father, "Glorify me . . . with the glory I had with you before the world began" (John 17:5). After he was raised from the dead, he *got* his glory back. "His head and hair were . . . as white as snow, and his eyes were like blazing fire. His feet were like bronze glowing in a furnace, and his voice was like the sound of rushing waters. . . . His face was like the sun shining in all its brilliance" (Revelation 1:14–16).

## Proof That Jesus Resurrected

All through this book we've talked about miracles. Some of them are done in a quiet way and could be explained away as a coincidence of natural phenomena. But as we've seen, *some* miracles God does are impossible to explain away. Jesus being raised from the dead is one of those undeniable miracles. All serious historians agree that Jesus was a real person who was crucified and died. The Roman soldiers reported that Jesus was dead. But *then* what happened?

- After three days God's Spirit raised Jesus back to life. His tomb was empty—even Jesus' enemies admitted that!
- The religious leaders gave the Roman guards money to tell this lie: "Jesus' disciples came during the night and stole his body while we slept." *Slept?* No way! Since the Roman soldiers were still alive to spread this rumor, it was obviously a lie. Roman guards didn't dare sleep on the job! The punishment was death.

- Jesus' grave clothes were empty, as if he had passed right through them.
- Jesus appeared to his disciples and ate food with them. He invited them to touch him, to convince them that he wasn't just a phantom.
- More than five hundred people said that Jesus appeared to them alive!
- The disciples changed from timid men hiding from the authorities to bold men who suffered beatings and death, because they believed that Jesus rose from the dead. If they were just making up a *story* about Jesus being alive, would they have been willing to *die* for that? Surely not.

**God has done** many, many miracles since the dawn of time. The creation of the earth and a *billion* galaxies was the first miracle and clearly a really big one. During the past few thousand years, God has continued to perform miracles. For him miracles are nothing unusual. They're just "business as usual." That's why the apostle Paul asked, "Why should any of you consider it incredible that God raises the dead?" (Acts 26:8).

Jesus was God's Son who came down from heaven and lived as a man on earth. He performed many miracles to prove to people he was the Messiah, but the greatest miracle was how much he *loved* us. He knew we were lost without God, and he died to pay the price for our sins. Then, three days later, one of the most astonishing of all miracles occurred—God raised him from the dead. With this act Jesus defeated the Devil, sin, and death. Now *that's* incredible!

You can plug into Jesus' miracle-working power by opening your heart and asking Jesus to come into your life and save you. "If you confess with your mouth, 'Jesus is Lord,' and believe in your heart that God raised him from the dead, you will be saved" (Romans 10:9).

GET DEEPER

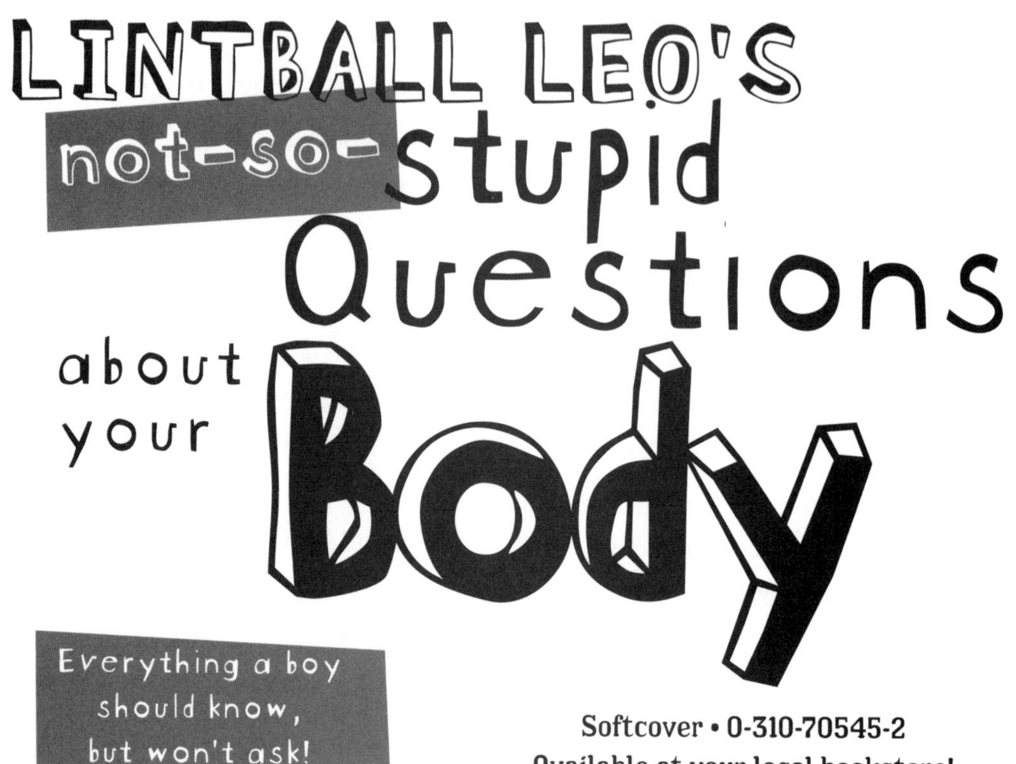
LINTBALL LEO'S
not-so-stupid
Questions
about your
Body
Everything a boy should know, but won't ask!
Softcover • 0-310-70545-2
Available at your local bookstore!

Now pay attention.
You just might learn something!

Chapter 1

# The Good, the Bad, and the Ugly?

"Ouch! That hurts," cried a tiny, mysterious voice from the piece of bellybutton lint Steve held between his fingers. "You want a piece of me? I'm not afraid of you!"

Steve hurried to his desk and picked up the magnifying glass he used to examine bugs. He looked carefully at the talking piece of lint that was now yelling like a squashed cat. Steve released his pinching grip and the piece of lint brushed himself off, fixed his hair, and fluffed out the finger squeeze marks from his stomach.

"Who are you?" asked Steve.

"I'm Lintball Leo, at your service," Leo answered taking a bow.

"Wow, a talking piece of lint. I must be dreaming," said Steve.

"This is no dream. Here. I'll pinch you." Leo tried to pinch Steve's hand, but his fingers were so small that Steve didn't feel a thing."

"Did you feel that?" asked Leo.

Not wanting to be impolite, Steve said, "That was some pinch. I guess I'm not dreaming after all."

Leo flexed his muscles. "I work out and eat only good, nutritious stuff. Gotta stay strong, you know."

"How long have you been living in my belly button?" Steve asked.

"Oh, I've been around for a few years now. Sometimes when you tried to clean your bellybutton, you knocked me down to other parts of your body," Leo told Steve. "I visited your feet once, and while it was nice to see my relatives who live down between your toes, I think I'd rather live in your bellybutton."

"Uh . . . I have things living between my toes?" asked Steve, looking a little nervous.

Relax! You're not going to turn into a big hairy monster... ...overnight!

"Relax, Steve. It's no big deal. All guys have a little extra dirt here and there. Hey! I've been most everywhere on your body, and I'm becoming an expert in boy-body anatomy. I'll be hanging around until you reach puberty. Then you won't need me anymore and I'll find another boy's bellybutton to call home."

"Puberty," said Steve. "I've heard that word

"Jesus grew in...stature, and in favor with God and men." Luke 2:52

before. Can you tell me what it means?"

"No problem." Leo drew himself up to his full fluffy height. "Puberty sounds like a strange word, but it's something that happens to all people. Puberty happens when young bodies start to change and mature—from boys into men, from girls into women.

Puberty?

Steve had a look of horror on his face.

"What's with the face? Don't panic! Puberty doesn't mean you're going to start shaving next week. It just means that most people begin to change into adults somewhere between the ages of nine and fifteen. And it doesn't happen all at once. Puberty can last anywhere from two to four years."

"That long?" asked Steve.

"Ah, it goes fast. Especially when you start thinking about *girls.*"

Steve blushed bright red.

"Puberty can be a pretty confusing time," Leo said. "But it helps if you remember it's all part of growing up. God made your body and this is the way he wants it to work—so don't sweat it."

"What if I don't *want* to go through puberty?" asks Steve.

"Unfortunately, that's not an option," Leo sighed. "When the time is right for you, it will just happen.

Then, you'll become a man. That's the good news."

"How old are you?" Steve tried to get a better look at Leo. Are you older than dirt?"

"Very funny, Steve. Let me give you some advice. I've been here and there over the years, and I've seen the good, the bad, and the ugly."

"*Now* you're talking about girls." Steve joked.

"Hey, another funny one. No, I'm not talking about girls. I'm talking about boys and how puberty affects them."

Steve looked worried. "Will this puberty thing hurt? I mean should I wear a helmet?"

With that Lintball Leo rolled up into a ball and

## Get Smarter

Growing up isn't easy to do. It would be less complicated if there were a training manual telling you what to expect throughout puberty. But we don't have a manual, and even if we did, everybody grows at a different pace and in a different way. Get smart by finding an older male you can talk to. The best person would be your dad. If he's not available, consider a youth pastor or counselor at your school. Ask very specific questions about growing up. Listen carefully to the answers. Then ask God to help you.

began laughing hysterically. “A helmet! That’s very funny! Ha ha ha . . .”

“Uh, Mr. Leo, when you get through laughing, do you think I could ask you some questions about my body?” Steve asked. “I’ve been too embarrassed to ask my parents or teachers. What do you say? Could you help me out?”

“Why certainly,” said Lintball Leo. “But you’ll have to promise that you’ll stop calling me Mr. Leo. (Whispering.) *That makes me sound so old.* Please, just call me Lintball.”

“OK, Lintball, I’ll do that,” Steve said with a smile.

“So shoot, Steve? You can ask me anything.”

Chapter 2

# I'm Not Liking My Body

"Yum, yum, this grape tastes great!" Leo said, as he wiped grape juice from his chin. "You like grapes, Steve?"

Steve thought for a moment and answered. "Yeah, I guess so. Grapes are okay, but my favorite fruit is the banana," he said.

Lintball Leo started laughing again. "Ha, ha, that's 'ripe,'" he said.

Steve looked puzzled. "Hey, what's so funny about a banana?"

Leo stopped laughing and answered. "Well a banana comes in

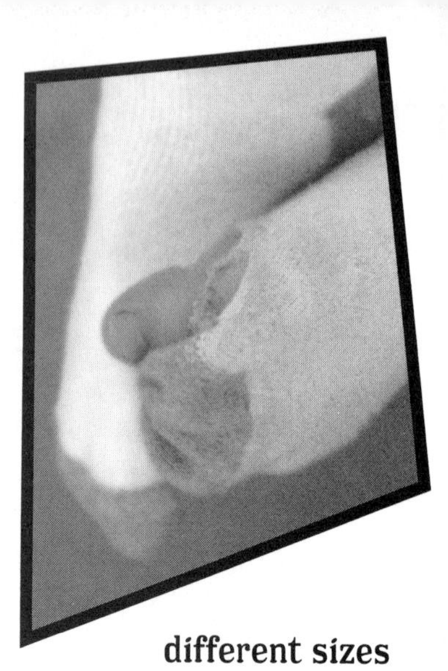

different sizes and changes colors faster than most boys change their socks."

Steve thought about that for a moment and agreed. "Yeah, you're right. When my mom brings bananas home from the supermarket, they're usually green. But within a few days, they change colors—and sometimes I'm still wearing the same pair of socks!" Steve laughed and then got serious.

"Hey Lintball, when you think about it, bananas

are lucky," he said.

Lintball Leo looked puzzled and asked, "How do you figure?"

Steve thought for a moment before answering. "Well, they get to change their looks from a green skin to a yellow skin. And when they change, people like them better," he said.

"Of course, then they end up being eaten," Lintball answered.

"I praise you because I am wonderfully made."
Psalm 139:14

"Good point," said Steve. "But sometimes I don't like my body, and I wish I could change it."

"Your concerns are perfectly normal, Steve. Most young boys have times when they don't like their bodies," Lintball told him.

"Yeah, I suppose," Steve didn't sound convinced.

Lintball continued. "Remember, Steve, that God designed boys to become men—to be masculine. So it's normal to be concerned about your body and how it looks. There are times when growing from a boy into a man can be embarrassing with so many physical changes beginning to take place."

"Yeah. I know I have to change or stay a kid forever. But sometimes I just look in the mirror and get disgusted with what I see," said Steve.

Lintball Leo gave Steve a reassuring pat on his thumb. "Steve, part of becoming a real man is learning to trust that God is in control and his ways are better than your ways. It's perfectly normal to wonder if God knows what he's doing. Just remember that the Bible says God designed you even while you were still in your mother's womb (Psalm 139:13). He has made you to be completely unique. No one in the history of mankind will have your fingerprints or your DNA or even your personality."

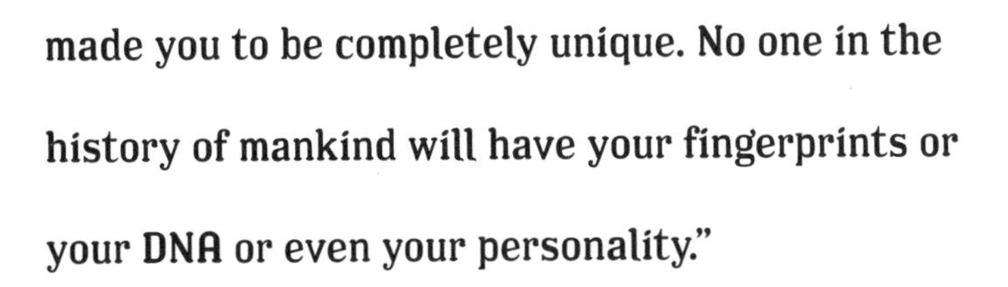

Steve smiled a little. He began to feel better about himself.

Lintball continued, "All boys experience physical changes in their bodies at different times. There is

Based on Luke 2:52:
"And Jesus grew in wisdom and stature,
and in favor with God and men (NIV)."

2:52 is designed just for boys 8-12!
This verse is one of the only verses in
the Bible that provides a glimpse of Jesus
as a young boy. Who doesn't wonder what
Jesus was like as a kid?

Become smarter, stronger, deeper,
and cooler as you develop
into a young man of God
with 2:52 Soul Gear™!

smarter•stronger
2:52
deeper•cooler
TM

Zonderkidz

The 2:52 Soul Gear™ takes a closer look by focusing on the four major areas of development highlighted in Luke 2:52:

"Wisdom" = mental/emotional = **Smarter**

"Stature" = physical = **Stronger**

"Favor with God" = spiritual = **Deeper**

"Favor with man" = social = **Cooler**

We want to hear from you. Please send your comments about this book to us in care of the address below. Thank you.

Zonderkidz®

*Grand Rapids, MI 49530*
*www.zonderkidz.com*